# FROSTY

## IS A

## STUPID

## NAME

*story by* TROY WILSON

*illustrations by* DEAN GRIFFITHS

ORCA BOOK PUBLISHERS

Frosty is a stupid name for a snowman.
At least that's what Jenny Fry thinks.
It's like naming a dog Furry.
Or naming a fish Wetty.
Or naming a slug Slimy.
Jenny won't settle for just any stupid name.

Her snowman deserves a good name.

No, a great name.

A name worth repeating down through the ages.

So Jenny sits.

She stands.

She paces back and forth.

Some names are too long.
Some names are too short.
Too hot.
Or too cold.
And then, one name is just right.

"Bartholomew," she tells him.
"Bartholomew Hatley Fry.
That's your name."

Bartholomew doesn't react at all.

"Oh, I'm sorry," Jenny says.
"How rude of me.
I forgot your hat."

She places it on his head, and he begins to dance around.

He's a much better dancer than that silly old Frosty.

He shakes and he shimmies.

He leaps and he twirls.

He glides through the air like a snowflake.

A man with a big black mustache
gives Jenny his card.
He wants to be Bartholomew's agent.
He wants to make Bartholomew a star.

"We'll get back to you," she says.
"Right now we're going to the Unicorn Planet."

Bartholomew and Jenny hop into
their spaceship and blast out of the
earth's atmosphere.

As they touch down on the Unicorn Planet,
Jenny rips up the man's card.

"I'm the only agent you'll ever need,"
she tells Bartholomew.

They each mount a unicorn and ride
through forests of cotton candy.
They ride along rivers of chocolate.
They ride for days.

They reach the royal palace just in time
for the Feast of Sweets.
They sit with the royal family.
And, even better, they gobble up as much
dessert as their bodies can hold.
It isn't until Jenny's tenth helping of
jelly-bean soup that it hits her.

She looks out at Bartholomew as he
dances with the queen.
And she wonders.
Is Bartholomew really having any fun?

After all, she's got a huge imagination.
She can see all kinds of things.
Spaceships, unicorns, palaces—you name it.
But Bartholomew? She isn't so sure.
Maybe all he sees is the front yard.
And the driveway.
And the house across the street.

Well, Jenny thinks, that's different.
And she gulps down her last jelly bean
before the palace fades away.

"Time for some real food," she declares, and she marches into the house.
A few minutes later, she struts back outside with four
peanut-butter-and-jelly sandwiches on a platter.
They look a little rough around the edges,
but Jenny's quite sure that Bartholomew doesn't notice.
They are, after all, his very first peanut-butter-and-jelly sandwiches.

Bartholomew doesn't have a throat, so Jenny digs a hole in his
belly and sticks two sandwiches inside.
Then she covers them up.

"Don't worry," she says between mouthfuls. "You're not missing much. Chewing is overrated. And anyway, peanut butter sticks to the roof of your mouth. See?" She opens her mouth as wide as she can and points to all the peanut butter stuck inside it.

"We have to let our food settle," she tells Bartholomew, "so we can't run around right now. But you know what I think? I think we should have a fashion show. You snowmen never get to dress up."

Jenny drags box after box of Dad's old clothes outside.
Then she dresses Bartholomew.
With every new outfit she holds up a mirror so he can see himself.
She tells him he looks great, even when he doesn't.

Then, just as Jenny drapes a housecoat over Bartholomew,
a snowball smacks him right between the eyes.
Kyle. Jenny's little brother Kyle.
Giggling that sneaky little giggle of his.
A second snowball slams into Bartholomew's belly.
A third ricochets off his side.
Jenny opens her mouth to call Mom, but then closes it.

She scoops up some snow,
crushes it into a ball and whips it at Kyle.
She misses.
He runs.
She hurls another and nails him right in the butt.
He disappears around the corner before she can throw again.

"That's why I didn't make a little brother for you," Jenny groans.
"They're nothing but trouble."

She cleans Bartholomew up.

"You know," she says, watching for Kyle, "this might be
a good time to get away from it all. We need a vacation."

She loads Bartholomew onto her sled
and pulls him around the block.
She points out all the sights along the way.
The creepy vacant lot.
Her best friend Amber's house.
Graffiti at the bus stop.
Everything.

After supper, Jenny shuffles outside with her schoolbooks and plops down beside Bartholomew. "I hate bringing work home with me," she says. "You're lucky. You'll never get homework." Between questions she shows him her paintings from art class.

Finally, it's time for bed.

Jenny lays Bartholomew down, turns on her flashlight and reads him a story.

Then she reads him another. And another.

She makes sure he has plenty of time to look at the pictures.

She closes the last book.

Tomorrow is a school day. It's supposed to get warmer.

Bartholomew will melt, but she doesn't tell him that.

There's no point in giving him nightmares.

In her imagination, Jenny can hear him talk. "Thank you," he says.
"Thank you for giving me the best day a snowman has ever had."
But he doesn't say that at all. He doesn't say anything.
Maybe he doesn't think anything, either.
Or maybe he thinks all snowmen eat peanut-butter-and-jelly sandwiches.
Maybe he thinks all snowmen go on holidays.
And maybe that's just as well.

Jenny covers his eyes with snow eyelids.
She gives him a hug.
"Good night," she says.
Good-bye, she thinks.

When she's back inside the warm house,
her eyes melt, just a little.
She dreams of the Unicorn Planet.
And she dances with Bartholomew until morning.

To the Greater Victoria Public Library system,
for their computers, printers and support.
To Mom and Dad, for their patience, love and support.
And to Frosty, whose name isn't really so stupid. —*T.W.*

To Troy's brain. —*D.G.*

Text copyright © 2005 Troy Wilson

Illustrations copyright © 2005 Dean Griffiths

**National Library of Canada Cataloguing in Publication Data:**

Wilson, Troy, 1970-

Frosty is a stupid name / story by Troy Wilson; illustrations by Dean Griffiths.

ISBN 1-55143-382-6

I. Griffiths, Dean, 1967- II. Title.

PS8645.I47F76 2005          jC813'.6          C2005-902259-0

First published in the United States 2005

**Library of Congress Control Number: 2005925270**

**Summary**: A young girl tries to give a snowman a special day on his terms rather than hers.

Orca Book Publishers gratefully acknowledges the support for its publishing programs
provided by the following agencies: the Government of Canada through the Book Publishing Industry
Development Program (BPIDP), the Canada Council for the Arts, and the British Columbia Arts Council.

Design and typesetting by Lynn O'Rourke
Interior and cover artwork created in watercolors.
Scanning by Island Graphics, Victoria, British Columbia

Orca Book Publishers
Box 5626 Stn. B
Victoria, BC  Canada
V8R 6S4

Orca Book Publishers
PO Box 468
Custer, WA   USA
98240-0468

Printed and bound in Hong Kong
09 08 07 06 05 • 5 4 3 2 1